The Cat Book

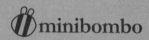 minibombo

First published 2017 by Walker Books Ltd, 87 Vauxhall Walk, London SE11 5HJ • This edition published 2019 • Copyright © 2013 minibombo/TIWI s.r.l. • English language translation © 2017 Walker Books Ltd • First published 2013 by minibombo, Italy as *Il libro gatto* by Silvia Borando • Published in the English language by arrangement with minibombo, an imprint of TIWI s.r.l., Via Emilia San Pietro, 25, 42121 Reggio Emilia, Italy • minibombo is a trademark of TIWI s.r.l. © 2013 minibombo/TIWI s.r.l. The moral rights of the author have been asserted • This book has been typeset in Tisa Pro Regular and Medium • Printed in China
• British Library Cataloguing in Publication Data: a catalogue record for this book is available from the British Library • ISBN 978-1-4063-8417-8 • **www.walker.co.uk** • 10 9 8 7 6 5 4 3 2 1

WALKER BOOKS
AND SUBSIDIARIES
LONDON • BOSTON • SYDNEY • AUCKLAND

MIX
Paper from
responsible sources
FSC™ C020056

Check out **www.minibombo.com**
to find plenty of fun ideas for playing
and creating – all inspired by this book!

Jan '19

020 835 800

Th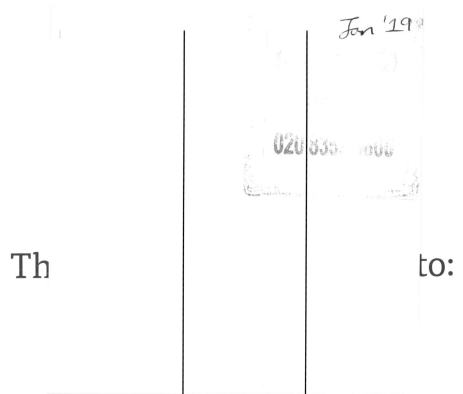to:

I'll call my cat:

Funny

Zzz zzz

Who's that curled in a ball?
Hey, sleepy cat, it's time to get up!
Can you help wake him?
Call out his name
and then turn the page.

Meoooow!

What a stretch!
Now he's wide awake.
Just look at him twitch
his tiny nose!
He wants you to pet him.
Softly stroke his back
and then turn the page.

Purr purr purr

Do you hear that?
He's purring!
Go on, make him purr even louder
with a little tickle under the chin.

Ahhh ... that makes
your cat so happy!
But what are those things
hopping on his tummy?
Fleeeeeas!
Quick, quick,
squish them with your finger
and then turn the page!

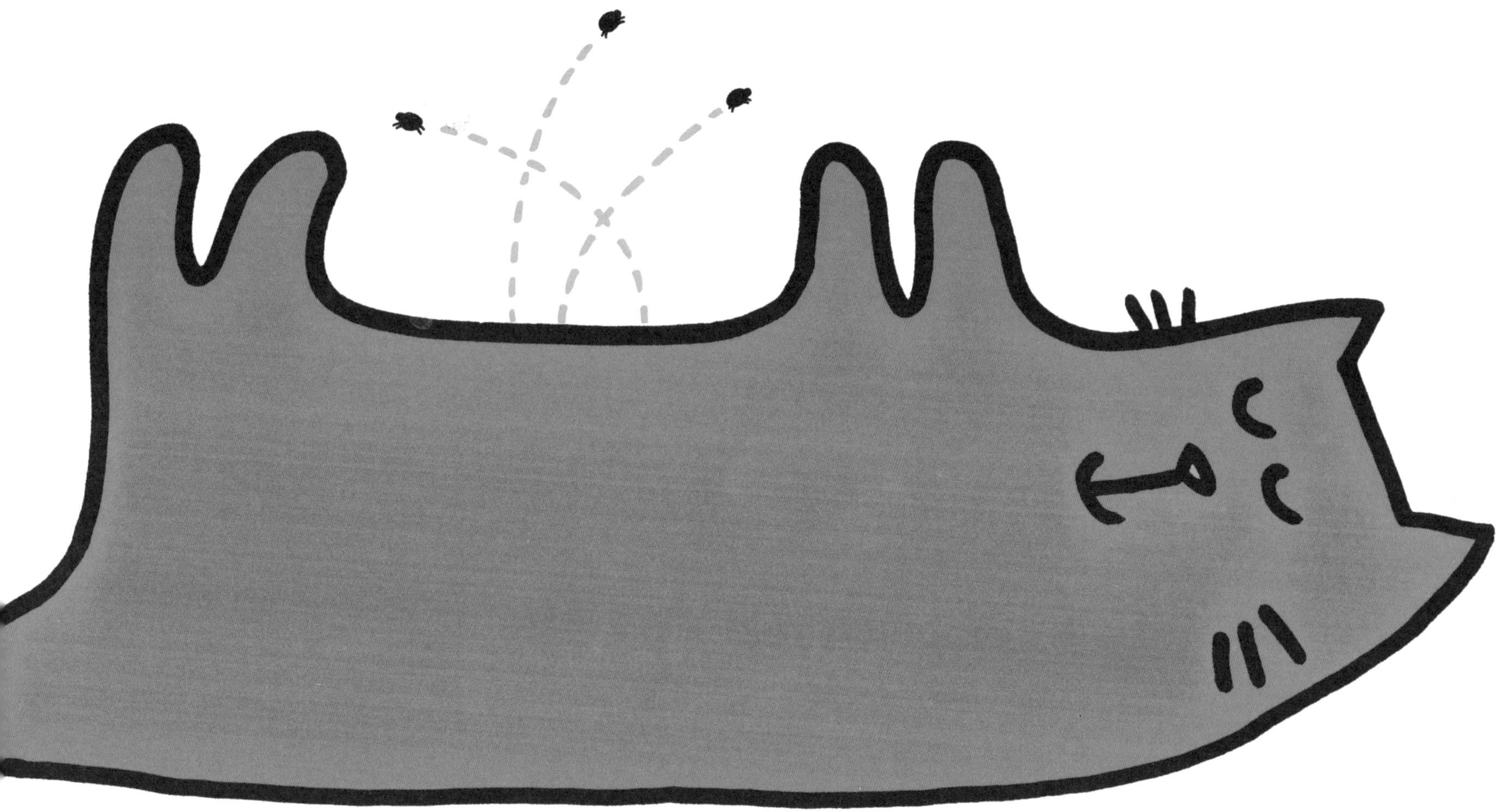

Good job, flea-squisher.
You got every single one!
Now, to finish the job,
take a big breath in
and blow them all away.
Whooooosh!

Phew! Flea emergency over.
But wait, was that a raindrop?
Uh-oh.
Don't let your cat get wet!
Shelter him with your hand
and then turn the page.

You made a great umbrella ...
but your cat still got a bit wet.
In fact, he got *very* wet.
What a soggy kitty!
Use your shirt as a towel
to give him a good rub.

Wow.
You've dried him
as dry as can be.
He's SO fluffy!
Smooth him down a bit
and then turn the page.

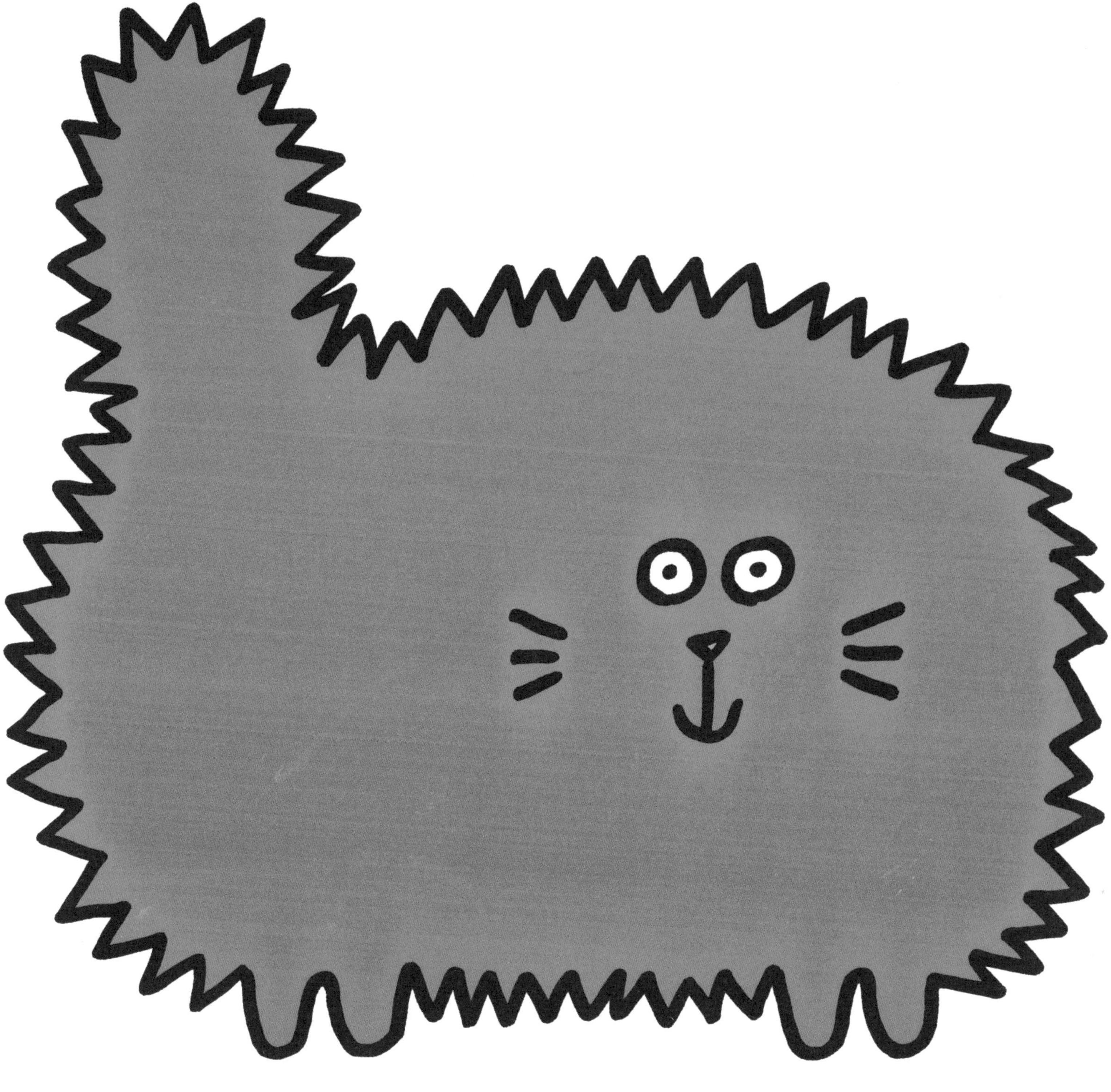

Yes, much better.
Oh! Look who's here –
a little bird!

Fly, bird, fly!
The cat will eat you for lunch.

Clap your hands and
make some noise
so the bird will
fly away!

Cat! What's that in your mouth?
Oh no, he caught the little bird!
But there might still be time.
Quick, give your cat's cheeks
a squeeze!

Hooray, the bird has flown away!
But now your cat is pretty tired.
It's been quite a busy day, after all.
Wish him a good night
with a little scratch
behind the ears.

Then slowly, so very slowly,
turn the page.

Shhh!

He's asleep.
Good night, cat.
Sleep tight.

Discover more minibombo books!

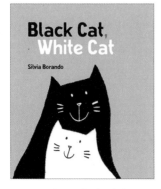

978-1-4063-6316-6

978-1-4063-6317-3

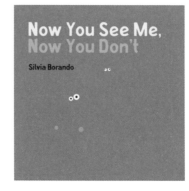

978-1-4063-6421-7

978-1-4063-6318-0

978-1-4063-6733-1

978-1-4063-6734-8

978-1-4063-7214-4

978-1-4063-6744-7

Available from all good booksellers

www.walker.co.uk